Migrant Youth
Falling Between the Cracks

Title List

Getting Ready for the Fair: Crafts, Projects, and Prize-Winning Animals

Growing Up on a Farm: Responsibilities and Issues

Migrant Youth: Falling Between the Cracks

Rural Crime and Poverty: Violence, Drugs, and Other Issues

Rural Teens and Animal Raising: Large and Small Pets

Rural Teens and Nature: Conservation and Wildlife Rehabilitation

Rural Teens on the Move:
Cars, Motorcycles, and Off-Road Vehicles

Teen Life Among the Amish and Other Alternative Communities:
Choosing a Lifestyle

Teen Life on Reservations and in First Nation Communities:
Growing Up Native

Teen Minorities in Rural North America: Growing Up Different

Teens and Rural Education: Opportunities and Challenges

Teens and Rural Sports: Rodeos, Horses, Hunting, and Fishing

Teens Who Make a Difference in Rural Communities: Youth Outreach
Organizations and Community Action

Migrant Youth
Falling Between the Cracks

by Joyce Libal

Mason Crest Publishers

Philadelphia

Mason Crest Publishers Inc.
370 Reed Road
Broomall, Pennsylvania 19008
(866) MCP-BOOK (toll free)
www.masoncrest.com

First printing
1 2 3 4 5 6 7 8 9 10
ISBN 978-1-4222-0011-7 (series)

Library of Congress Cataloging-in-Publication Data

Libal, Joyce.
   Migrant youth : falling between the cracks / by Joyce Libal.
      p. cm. — (Youth in rural North America)
   Includes bibliographical references (p. 93) and index.
   ISBN 978-1-4222-0020-9
   1. Child migrant agricultural laborers—United States—Social condi-
tions—Juvenile literature. 2. Child migrant agricultural laborers—
Canada—Social conditions—Juvenile literature. I. Title. II. Series.
   HD1525.L53 2007
   331.3'830869120973—dc22

                              2005033399

Cover and interior design by MK Bassett-Harvey.
Produced by Harding House Publishing Service, Inc.
www.hardinghousepages.com

Cover image design by Peter Spires Culotta.
Cover photography by iStock Photography (Vladimirs Prusakovs,
   Alex Bramwell, and Nancy Nehring).
Printed in Malaysia by Phoenix Press.

Contents

Introduction

by Celeste Carmichael

Results of a survey published by the Kellogg Foundation reveal that most people consider growing up in the country to be idyllic. And it's true that growing up in a rural environment does have real benefits. Research indicates that families in rural areas consistently have more traditional values, and communities are more closely knit. Rural youth spend more time than their urban counterparts in contact with agriculture and nature. Often youth are responsible for gardens and farm animals, and they benefit from both their sense of responsibility and their understanding of the natural world. Studies also indicate that rural youth are more engaged in their communities, working to improve society and local issues. And let us not forget the psychological and aesthetic benefits of living in a serene rural environment!

The advantages of rural living cannot be overlooked—but neither can the challenges. Statistics from around the country show that children in a rural environment face many of the same difficulties that are typically associated with children living in cities, and they fare worse than urban kids on several key indicators of positive youth development. For example, rural youth are more likely than their urban counterparts to use drugs and alcohol. Many of the problems facing rural youth are exacerbated by isolation, lack of jobs (for both parents and teens), and lack of support services for families in rural communities.

When most people hear the word "rural," they instantly think "farms." Actually, however, less than 12 percent of the population in rural areas make their livings through agriculture. Instead, service jobs are the top industry in rural North America. The lack of opportunities for higher paying jobs can trigger many problems: persistent poverty, lower educational standards, limited access to health care, inadequate housing, underemployment of teens, and lack of extracurricular possibilities. Additionally, the lack of—or in some cases surge of—diverse populations in rural communities presents its own set of challenges for youth and communities. All these concerns lead to the greatest threat to rural communities: the mass exodus of the post–high school population. Teens relocate for educational, recreational, and job opportunities, leaving their hometown indefinitely deficient in youth capital.

This series of books offers an in-depth examination of both the pleasures and challenges for rural youth. Understanding the realities is the first step to expanding the options for rural youth and increasing the likelihood of positive youth development.

CHAPTER 1
Who Are the Migrants of North America?

The jar of picanté sauce rolled along the bottom of the cart as Julia reached for a can of green beans. After quickly scanning the list her mother had pressed into her palm earlier that day, Julia pushed the cart toward produce and was again annoyed by the wheel that slid sideways along the linoleum. Once in the produce section, she selected apples, onions, lettuce, and **cilantro**. *Just grape juice, milk, and butter left, and I'm out of here, she thought.*

9

Julia was glad the total of her purchases came to less than the money her mom had given her, because she was allowed to keep the change. Like most of us, she never gave a thought to the people who grew the food that fed her family, how the food made it from field to store, or why it didn't cost more.

By the time Julia headed home, it was almost dark, but she could still see the fields and orchards that were part of the landscape near her Oregon home. Julia remembered people had been in the fields that morning, but she didn't know who they were or understand what they actually did. She certainly didn't realize all the foods she purchased that day were the products of farmworkers' labor. Nor did she consider the difficult nature of farm labor or the price that's paid by those who do it. Julia did, however, believe certain *stereotypes* regarding migrant workers.

Stereotype 1:

ALL WORKERS IN THE AGRICULTURAL FIELDS OF NORTH AMERICA ARE MIGRANTS

Most farmworkers in the United States and Canada are not migrants. More than 40 percent of American farmworkers are not classified as migrants because they do not travel far enough for work to make it necessary to spend the night away from home. They may live in areas that allow them to find agricultural work for the entire year, or they are able to find other employment for part of the year.

The term "migrant" is used to describe workers who travel many miles from their permanent place of residence. Those who travel seventy-five miles or less from their homes are often referred to as "shuttle migrants." These workers, about 39 percent of migrant farmworkers, often return to their homes in the evening. Only 17

Farmworkers in Gilroy, California, harvest yellow peppers. Some of these workers will follow the crops, going wherever there is a harvest, but others will stay in one place, doing whatever work is needed on the region's farms.

percent of farmworkers are migrants who "follow the crops" and remain away from their homes while doing that. "Settled out" is a term often used to describe former migrant families that are no longer traveling great distances from home to do agricultural work.

Opinions differ on exactly how many migrant farmworkers there are in the United States and Canada. According to the U.S. Department of Health and Human Services:

• There are between three and five million migrant farmworkers in American fields annually. (It is difficult to obtain precise statistics regarding this element of the population. According to the U.S. Department of Labor, approximately 800,000 to 900,000 people work as migrant farmworkers.

Cornell University puts it at between one and three million. Discrepancies among government sources and other agencies occur for several reasons. Undocumented workers are reluctant to complete forms that could lead to **deportation**. As workers move from one state to another, they may be counted in more than one location. Various agencies may be defining the term "migrant" in different ways.)

• The average income of migrant farmworkers is less than $7,500 annually. (According to the most recent National Agricultural Workers Survey [NAWS], 50 percent of individual farmworkers earn less than $7,500, while 75 percent of farmworker families have combined incomes of less than $10,000 per year. The U.S. Department of Health and Human Services places the 2005 poverty guideline at $19,350 for a family of four.)

• Most adult migrant farmworkers have had six years of schooling. (This is the usual amount of schooling achieved by workers entering the migrant workforce from Mexico. However, 15 percent of all farmworkers have completed twelve or more years of school.)

• The majority of migrant farmworkers are under thirty-five years old. (The National Agricultural Workers Survey places the average age at thirty-one, but also says half of all farmworkers are under twenty-one. Seven percent are between the ages of fourteen and seventeen.)

• Sixty-six percent of migrant farmworkers who are parents travel with their children. (According to the National Center for Farmworker Health, Inc., "an estimated 250,000 children migrate with their parents each year." Just as discrepancies occur between organizations estimating the number of migrant farmworkers in the nation, they also occur regarding the number of migrating children.)

Stereotype 2:

ALL MIGRANT WORKERS WHO ARE FROM ANOTHER COUNTRY ARE IN THE UNITED STATES ILLEGALLY

Some farmworkers in the United States are U.S. citizens, but most follow-the-crop and shuttle migrants are foreign born. Political unrest and economic difficulties in other countries encourage some residents of those countries to seek agricultural employment in North America. Most of these individuals are striving to create a better life for themselves and their families. Some, unable to obtain legal permission to cross into North America to work, do so illegally. According to the National Agricultural Workers Survey, of the farmworkers questioned, 22 percent were citizens, 24 percent were legal permanent residents, 2 percent had temporary work permits, and 52 percent lacked work authorization.

Stereotype 3:

MOST MEXICAN AMERICANS ARE MIGRANT FARMWORKERS OR MEMBERS OF FAMILIES THAT ONCE WERE

Nothing could be further from the truth. As of 2003, America had a Hispanic population of 39.9 million. The vast majority of this population group works in areas other than agriculture.

Some of these workers picking strawberries may be black, Asian, white, Native American, and Hispanic.

Stereotype 4:

ALL MIGRANT FARMWORKERS ARE FROM MEXICO

Nearly 90 percent of migrant farmworkers are Hispanic; but Caucasians, American Indians, African Americans, and people from the Caribbean and Southeast Asia are also farm laborers. At various times in U.S. history, Chinese, Japanese, and others have been largely represented in the migrant labor force as well.

Stereotype 5:

ALL MIGRANT FAMILIES ARE HOMELESS

This is not the case. Many have permanent homes in the southern part of the country, and 42 percent have homes outside of the United States. Many migrant families live in Texas, California, or Florida. Often their homes are located in areas where adult family members are not able to obtain yearlong employment. Other times, they are unable to find employment that pays well enough to support their families throughout the year. In this case, having many hands available for agricultural work (in other words, allowing their children to participate in farm labor) may make it economically attractive to migrate away from home for several months each year.

Canada's Migrant Agricultural Workers

Not much statistical information is available on migrant agricultural workers in Canada. Seasonal agricultural employment does exist in the provinces, but exactly how many workers move from one area to another to do this work is not clear.

Ontario is the main destination of nonresident agricultural workers who are admitted under Canada's temporary worker program Commonwealth Caribbean and Mexican Seasonal Agricultural Workers Program (CCMSAWP), begun in 1966. However, these migrant farmworkers also travel to Alberta, Manitoba, and Quebec. In 2002, 17,000 CCMSAWP workers were admitted. Fifty-five percent of them were from Mexico, and most of the remaining workers were from Jamaica.

How is "agriculture" defined when determining the eligibility of migrant children and youth for government programs?

Agriculture is defined as any activity directly related to the production or processing of crops, dairy products, poultry, or livestock. This includes preparing the soil, planting, cultivation, and harvesting of fruits and vegetables; production or processing of milk products and meat animals; and raising or gathering eggs. "Processing" refers to refining agricultural or fishing products. Migrant agricultural workers are employed in canning plants as well as in poultry- and other meat- and fish-processing facilities.

Canadian farmers often request the return of specific workers; the Mexican Ministry of Labor recruits others. Although the Canadian/Mexican Memorandum of Understanding regarding this program specifies workers be at least eighteen years old, the Mexican government requires them to be at least twenty-five. Only workers are admitted to the country under this program; family members do not receive visas.

One group of migrant workers annually enters Canada with family members: the *Mennonites*, most of whom come from Mexico, Paraguay, Bolivia, or Belize. They are able to enter Canada because they once lived in Canada and have maintained citizenship there. These Mennonite families often migrate together and are usually employed in Alberta, Manitoba, or Ontario. Some leave after every harvest, while others remain for a number of years.

The Need for Migrant Laborers

The demand for seasonal farmworkers in the United States and Canada is ongoing. Workers are routinely—though inconsistently—required to plant, thin, hoe, harvest, and process the foods we eat. When an agricultural job needs to be done, it often has to be accomplished on a scale too large for the local worker population to handle. Other times, farm owners wish to accomplish it at a cost below what the local population would accept as payment. This creates an opportunity for a mobile population of workers who move from one area to another, obtaining work at each location. Particularly in the United States, this population of workers often includes families with children.

CHAPTER 2
Youth on the Migrant Trail

Although he is only sixteen, Alejandro sometimes feels like a tired old man. He leaves school early every year for a summer of hard labor. Like most teenagers, he was happy when he got his driver's license, but there's no joy now as he shares driving duty with his father during their long trek north from Texas. Alejandro knows he'll be in the fields six days a week, and that some days, work will last from 6:30 A.M. until almost 8:00 P.M. When summer is over, his father will hand him a small amount of the money he's earned. The rest of Alejandro's earnings will be used to pay family bills throughout the winter.

"We go to the fields and weed and pick. It's hard because we don't eat until we get home. Sometimes I like for school vacation to be over so we don't have to go to the fields."

—an eleven-year-old migrant farmworker

Child Labor

Estimates of the number of children traveling the migrant labor circuit vary from 250,000 to one million. An international boundary is crossed by approximately 90,000 of them.

The number of migrant children working in farm labor each year range from an estimated 98,000 to 290,000. The National Children's Center for Rural and Agricultural Health and Safety places the number of fourteen- to seventeen-year-old migrant farmworkers at 128,000 and says, "The largest group of teen farmworkers working in crop production (47 percent) are economically independent (*emancipated minors*)." The NAWS reports that there are approximately 55,000 migrant youths traveling the migrant circuit unaccompanied by adults. Approximately two-thirds of the unaccompanied youths were born outside of the United States.

The Work Life of Migrant Families

For migrant families, summers are not reserved for vacations and an enjoyable three months off from school. For those big enough to work, every day can be long and exhausting. Often nightfall arrives before they can rest a short time with family (friends are usually hundreds of miles away). Families housed near each other in labor camps may spend a short amount of time socializing, but most will go to sleep relatively early because they need to rise in the predawn hours to prepare for return to the fields.

Farmworkers often do not have the luxury of a forty-hour work-week. The NAWS determined the majority work between thirty-one and fifty hours per week, with 15 percent working more than fifty hours. Their weekends are not always spared from labor. Many farm laborers work all day Saturday or a half-day on Saturday and per-haps Sunday. They may work from sunup to sundown, sometimes longer. These long hours can contribute to the physical danger of farm work; when workers are exhausted, accidents are more likely to occur.

Farm work is among the most dangerous in North America. Farm machinery, transportation, irrigation ditches, chemicals, and ani-mals all pose a threat to children. Approximately 104 children and youths under the age of twenty die from accidents on U.S. farms every year; more than 22,000 nonfatal injuries involve minors, ap-proximately 3.2 percent of which result in permanent disability. It is estimated that children under the age of sixteen compose up to 20 percent of farm deaths in both the United States and Canada. The middle years of adolescence and youngsters from toddlers through age four have the greatest risk of accidental *trauma* on farms.

Agricultural work is physically demanding, often requiring work-ers (including teens and younger workers) to lift forty- or fifty-pound sacks. Stooping, bending, and kneeling can be hard on young

Migrant Streams

Historically, migrant workers have traveled three main routes as they progressed along the agricultural circuit. These are still referred to as migrant streams. People in the "western stream" migrate north from California. Those in the "central stream" migrate north, northwest, and toward the Midwest from Texas. Migrant workers traveling along the "eastern stream" begin in Florida and work up the eastern seacoast as far as Maine and as far inland as Michigan.

backs and knees, especially when these motions must be repeated for many hours. Laborers work around dangerous machinery, and since they work in fields subject to the application of chemical fertilizers and pesticides, they risk exposure to these substances as well.

Child Labor Laws in the United States

Youth who participate in agricultural labor do not have the same legal protections as those who work in other areas. Legislation passed in 1974 makes it legal for teens at least fourteen years old to work in agricultural fields for an unlimited number of hours when school is not in session. Youth sixteen years old and above can legally handle pesticides and operate potentially hazardous equipment. Employers sometimes turn a blind eye toward younger children working in fields.

The Fair Labor Standards Act

The Fair Labor Standards Act of 1938 (FLSA) (as amended) governs child labor in agriculture. This federal law applies to "employees whose work involves production of agricultural goods which will leave the state directly or indirectly and become a part of interstate commerce." According to the FLSA:

- Youths ages sixteen and above may work in any farm job at any time.

- Youths ages fourteen and fifteen may work outside of school hours in jobs not declared hazardous by the secretary of labor.

- Youths ages twelve and thirteen may work outside of school hours in nonhazardous jobs on farms that also employ their parent(s) or with written parental consent.

- Youths less than age twelve may work outside of school hours in nonhazardous jobs with parental consent, but only on farms where none of the employees are subject to the minimum-wage requirements of the FLSA.

- Local youths ages ten and eleven may hand harvest short-season crops outside of school hours for no more than eight weeks between June 1 and October 15 if their employers have obtained special waivers from the secretary of labor.

Wages Earned

Sometimes migrant workers are paid an hourly wage. Even when they work more than forty hours a week, they rarely receive overtime pay. Other times, they are paid according to the number of pounds harvested, often called a piece-work rate. A study conducted by Human Rights Watch found some child farmworkers receiving only $2.50 or less per hour. Most youth doing agricultural labor in the United States earn between $1,000 and $2,500 annually.

- Youths of any age may work at any time in any job on a farm owned or operated by their parents.

  The secretary of labor has deemed the following agricultural jobs hazardous. Therefore, youths fifteen years old and younger may not legally perform these jobs. Those sixteen years old and above may perform any of these tasks:

- operating a tractor of over 20 PTO horsepower, or connecting or disconnecting an implement or any of its parts to or from such a tractor

- operating or working with a corn picker, cotton picker, grain combine, hay mower, forage harvester, hay baler, potato digger, mobile pea viner, feed grinder, crop dryer, forage blower, auger conveyor, unloading mechanism of a nongravity-type self-unloading wagon or trailer, power post-hole digger, power post driver, or nonwalking-type rotary tiller

- operating or working with a trencher or earthmoving equipment, fork lift, potato combine, or power-driven circular, band, or chain saw

- working in a yard, pen, or stall occupied by a bull, boar, or stud horse maintained for breeding purposes; a sow with suckling pigs; or a cow with a newborn calf (with umbilical cord present)

- felling, buckling, skidding, loading, or unloading timber with a butt diameter of more than 6 inches

- working from a ladder or scaffold at a height of over 20 feet

- driving a bus, truck, or automobile to transport passengers, or riding on a tractor as a passenger or helper

- working inside a fruit, forage, or grain storage designed to retain an oxygen-deficient or toxic atmosphere; an upright silo within two weeks after silage has been added or when a top unloading device is in operating position; a manure pit; or a horizontal silo while operating a tractor for packing purposes

- handling or applying toxic agricultural chemicals identified by the words "danger," "poison," or "warning," or a skull and crossbones on the label

- handling or using explosives

- transporting, transferring, or applying anhydrous ammonia

If you are sixteen years old or older, it is legal for you to perform all the tasks in this list. The regulations against youth ages fifteen and under engaging in these hazardous activities does not apply to teens who work on farms owned or operated by their parents. There are also two other exemptions:

- Youths who are fourteen- and fifteen-year-old student learners enrolled in vocational agricultural programs are exempt from the restrictions against certain hazardous occupations when certain requirements are met.

- Minors ages fourteen and fifteen who hold certificates of completion or training under a 4-H or vocational agriculture training program may work outside school hours on certain equipment for which they have been trained.

Many states have passed their own laws governing children and youths working in agriculture. In these states, whichever law (federal or state) is the strictest is the one that must be followed. Twenty-seven states restrict the number of hours per day and per week that can be worked by children and youth. Some states forbid them working during early morning or late evening hours.

Child Labor Laws in Canada

Canada also has laws governing minimum ages of children involved in agricultural employment and the types of work they can perform. In most Canadian provinces, child labor laws apply equally to agriculture and other types of employment. Ontario has established separate agricultural child labor statutes. In Manitoba, some provisions of laws prohibiting employment of children under age sixteen do not apply to agriculture unless the employment is such that "the safety, health, or well-being of the child is likely to be adversely affected or in an operation in which a substantive part of the work is done with machinery."

Strawberries are just one of the many fruits picked by migrant farmworkers, including youth and children.

Most Canadian provinces prohibit the employment of children during school hours. For example:

• In Alberta, children ages twelve through fourteen may work up to two hours outside of normal school hours or eight hours on nonschool days. Night work is prohibited.

• In New Brunswick, children under age sixteen can work no more than six hours on a nonschool day or three hours on a school day. Work and school combined cannot exceed eight hours. Night work is prohibited.

Wages in Ontario (in Canadian dollars)

According to the Ontario Ministry of Labour, students under age eighteen working as harvesters (a term used in Canada to describe farmworkers) received at least the minimum hourly rate of $7.75 per hour in 2006. By 2007, this will rise to $8.00 if they are employed more than twenty-eight hours per week during the school term. Students under age eighteen who are employed twenty-eight hours or less per week during the school term or who work during school holidays are entitled to receive the "student minimum wage." This amounts to $7.25 per hour in 2006, and will rise to $7.50 per hour by 2007.

- In Newfoundland, children under age sixteen can work no more than eight hours on a nonschool day or three hours on a school day. Work and school combined cannot exceed eight hours. Night work is prohibited.

- In Nova Scotia, children under age fourteen can work no more than eight hours on a nonschool day or three hours on a school day. Work and school combined cannot exceed eight hours. Night work is prohibited. Parents or guardians of children can be fined for not complying with the law.

- In Prince Edward Island, children under age sixteen can work no more than eight hours on a nonschool day or three hours on a school day. Night work is prohibited. The Prince Edward Island Youth Employment Act prohibits employment of young persons where a toxic substance or equipment or machinery is potentially dangerous to them.

Even when they are not laboring in agricultural fields, the health and safety of migrant children and youth can be at risk. Although the government has developed programs aimed at meeting their needs, these young people lag behind others in terms of medical care.

CHAPTER 3
Physical Health and Safety

Obituary, January 23, 2005

Jessica Govea Thorbourne died today of breast cancer at age fifty-eight. Ms. Thorbourne became a migrant worker in California at the age of four. Because she was not big enough to carry the large sack used by adults picking cotton, her mother made her a small sack that could hold twenty-five pounds (approximately 11 kilograms). Jessica grew up in the agricultural fields of North America. By the time she was twelve, she was already a political activist. As president of the Junior Community Service Organization, she led farmworker children in a petition drive to establish a local park. In her late teens, Jessica worked with César Chávez and helped organize the United Farm Workers (UFW). At twenty-one, she traveled to Toronto and Montreal, where she worked successfully to gain Canadian support for a boycott of California table grapes. She became the Canadian boycott director and the UFW's national organizing director, as well as the director of voter registration efforts and a member of the UFW's National Executive Board. She worked with leaders of a coffee processing workers' union in El Salvador and with other workers' unions. She served as the New Jersey state director of the National AFL-CIO and the state director of the Union Leadership Academy. Ms. Thorbourne went on to become a labor educator. She was a member of the faculty at Rutgers University and Cornell University and taught classes at other universities throughout the country. Her image is included on a mural on the Women's Building in San Francisco, and she was featured on the PBS programs *Chicano! The Mexican-American Civil Rights Movement* and *The Fight in the Fields*. She was an advocate on the issue of pesticide poisoning. Jessica Govea Thorbourne believed the cancer that killed her was caused by pesticide exposure she experienced while working as a migrant laborer throughout her childhood.

A Dangerous Occupation

Exposure to agricultural chemicals (including pesticides, *herbicides*, and *fungicides*) is just one of the hazards that make farm work one of the most dangerous occupations in North America. Accidents using simple equipment (such as falls from ladders) occur, as well as accidents involving large machinery. Migrant farmworkers are often not covered by workers' compensation. When one of these workers is hurt on the job, his family is impacted by the lack of income that results. Repetitive-motion injuries and strains caused by heavy lifting often lead to *chronic* health problems. While the life expectancy for North Americans has risen to over age seventy-five,

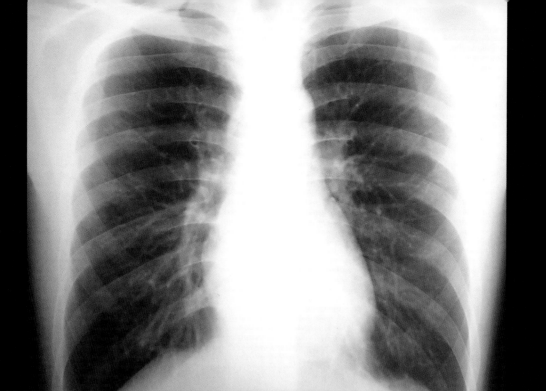

Tuberculosis is bacteria-caused disease that usually affects the lungs.

according to the Centers for Disease Control and Prevention, the life expectancy of farmworkers remains at just forty-nine.

According to the National Center for Farmworker Health, Inc. (NCFH), "The health of farmworker children is one of the poorest of any group in the country and is a major concern within the migrant health field." Two studies have shown 61 percent of migrant children with "at least one health problem" and 43 percent with "two or more." Another study showed 34 percent suffering from "intestinal parasites, severe asthma, chronic diarrhea, vitamin A deficiency, chemical poisoning or continuous *otitis media* leading to hearing loss." Estimates of the *infant mortality rate* among migrant farmworkers ranges from 25 to 125 percent above the national average.

Understanding Chemical Exposures

Regulations regarding pesticide hazards are determined by adult exposure; they do not give special consideration to children or youth. If a child and adult are standing next to each in a field and exposed to the same pesticide, the child will absorb more of the chemical per pound of body weight. This is because the child's body is smaller and children have a higher metabolism rate. The child is also still developing her body organs and central nervous system. Therefore, the pesticide poses a much greater hazard to her than to the adult.

Pesticide Exposure

More than a billion pounds of pesticides are applied to North American fields every year. Although laws prevent laborers from being forced to work in fields undergoing pesticide applications, children, youth, and adults are still at risk of exposure to these chemicals. In a survey performed in New York, 48 percent of migrant children reported working in agricultural fields wet with pesticides. Sprays can drift through the air and be ingested by people in nearby areas. In the same New York study, 36 percent of migrant children reported being directly sprayed with pesticides or having it drift onto them.

Chemical residues that remain on the plants and soil can be transferred to the skin of workers. Every year farmworkers develop rashes, burns, nausea, vomiting, eye problems, headaches, dizziness, and other discomforts and illnesses as a direct result of chemical exposure. Many also blame chronic illnesses on past exposures to pesticides. Asthma, liver and kidney diseases, neurological problems, and even cancers, sterility, and birth defects have been linked to these chemicals. Farmworkers—including children and youth—sometimes spend several days working in fields before they are informed of the risks posed by pesticides that have been used there. Between 1998 and 2001, skin rashes (one of the signs of pesticide exposure) doubled among farmworkers.

Problems of Dust

Naturally, people working in fruit and vegetable fields gather dirt, dust, and other agricultural residue on their clothing and bodies. This has the potential to harm their health in the immediate environment and when it is carried into their homes. There, it can affect young children who have not been to the fields. Along with damage that can be caused by ingesting these substances, babies' development can be affected. What's more, when floors accumulate this dust and also when living conditions are very crowded, parents are understandably reluctant to place infants on the floor. Babies who are not provided with enough floor exercise can have underdeveloped hip, leg, and neck muscles.

Danger Beyond the Fields

On November 13, 1999, more than two hundred people living in Earlimart, California, became ill after a soil fumigant called metam sodium (sold as Sectagon) was applied to a field south of the town. Some parts of the community had to be evacuated because of the gas cloud. A year later, over twenty adults and at least nine children remained ill with serious headaches and respiratory ailments.

Sanitation in the Fields

Guidelines issued in 1987 require that farmworkers have access to toilets, hand-washing facilities, and drinking water. These measures can limit prolonged exposure to pesticides on workers' skin and reduce risk of disease from unsanitary conditions. Unfortunately, these standards only apply to farms where eleven or more workers were employed to do hand labor during one day of the previous twelve months. Although conditions have been steadily improving, as late as 2003, 10 percent of farmworkers in the southeast still did not have easy access to toilets, and 18 percent did not have access to hand-washing facilities while working. Parasitic infections, hepatitis, and many other *communicable* diseases can be caused by unsanitary conditions.

In his book *Latino Migrant Workers: America's Harvesters*, author Christopher Hovius points out how an unscrupulous employer can circumvent sanitation laws:

> Sometimes employers will hire an entire family, but list only one member on its payroll. The entire earnings of the family are then paid out to the person on the payroll. . . . So while an employer might have 50 people working on any given day, the payroll might show merely 10 names. . . . Consequently, it appears as though the grower need not provide hand-washing and toilet facilities that the law requires for operations of 11 or more people.

Nutrition

Like others who live in poverty, migrant families sometimes struggle to provide a balanced diet for their children. Food stamps help alleviate this situation, and the Child Nutrition and WIC Reauthorization Act of 2004 makes migrant children and youth eligible for free school meals. Additionally, churches and other nonprofit organizations in many communities maintain food pantries or provide direct food aid to qualifying individuals, including migrant families. Still, many migrant children and youth do not have a balanced diet. This can lead to obesity, diabetes, cardiovascular disease, anemia, and dental problems.

Dental Care

Tooth decay and other oral health problems are common in the migrant community. According to the NCFH, "Dental disease ranks as one of the top five health problems for farmworkers ages 5 through 29. . . . For children ages 10 to 19, dental disease is the chief complaint." Children and youth with untreated tooth decay may be unable to chew their food well or to eat comfortably. They often suffer from persistent pain that interferes with schoolwork and other activities. Discolored, permanently damaged, and lost teeth can cause embarrassment and result in unfair treatment from others. One study of children of Mexican American farmworkers revealed only 46 percent had ever been to the dentist. A study conducted by the University of Michigan showed that 65 percent of the children of migrant farmworkers had tooth decay. This compares with 16 percent tooth decay in same-age children in the general population. The study also revealed a lower rate of treatment: 29 percent compared to 76 percent.

Among farmworkers, the most commonly cited reasons for not seeking dental care are "time" and "cost." In one study, 57 percent of the migrant workers questioned listed limited clinic hours as a deterrent to care. Those who speak English are more likely to seek dental services. Some dentists and nonprofit organizations provide free or low-cost dental services to migrant families, but these are not available everywhere they are needed.

Infectious Disease

Many people think of tuberculosis as a disease of the past, but Michigan experienced an outbreak in a migrant labor camp in 2002. Studies conducted in several states showed between 37 and 48 percent of migrant farmworkers tested showed a positive response for tuberculosis. Treatment of this disease takes six months. Language barriers between medical personnel and patients, coupled with the *transient* lifestyle of migrant farmworkers, can lead to some individuals stopping their medication before six months has elapsed. This

The large machinery used on farms is just one of the dangers farmworkers may face.

can cause the development of dangerous treatment-resistant strains of tuberculosis.

Vehicle and Equipment Safety

The economic situation of many migrant families can lead them to own or travel in older vehicles, some of which have safety issues. Sometimes families do not have car seats for all children requiring

Health Education

Organizations in many states are trying to improve the health of migrant family members through education. Healthy Living (<u>Vidas Sanas</u>) is one such program that has distributed information on mental health issues such as depression and substance abuse.

them. Even when car seats are available, they may not be used because of space limitations within the vehicle.

Obviously, farm machinery can pose a danger to young children. An article titled "They Harvest the Crops," published by *SIRS Digests* in spring 1997, told the story of a ten-year-old who spent a day in the fields, then fell asleep on a pile of burlap bags. According to the staff writer, workers did not notice the sleeping child as they added their own bags to the pile, covering her body. Later, someone drove a farm truck over the bags. The little girl's lifeless body was not discovered until the next day. Joel Compos suffered the same fate in 1992 when, exhausted from work, he fell asleep in an agricultural field in Washington. He was fourteen years old. Children too young to work in fields and left to entertain themselves may be injured by vehicles while playing in parking areas or other unsafe places.

Small children may not be noticed when they are sleeping in the fields. Without adequate supervision, there is a constant risk that a child may be injured or killed by the heavy harvesting machines.

The Migrant Health Act

In 1962, Congress passed the Migrant Health Act. Four years later, the Migrant Health Center Program, which provides health-related services to migrant families, was initiated by the U.S. Department of Health, Education, and Welfare. (In 1979, this department was divided in two: the Department of Education and the Department of Health and Human Services.)

The federal government often gives grants to nonprofit organizations to fund programs that provide needed services for migrant families. Migrant Head Start is an example. Because it is usually

Dangerous Health Practices

To keep themselves healthy and reduce the cost of health care, some migrant workers purchase vitamins, antibiotics, and other classified medications in Mexico and U.S. areas along the Mexican border. This is done without consulting a doctor or obtaining a prescription. Sometimes needles and syringes used to self-administer drugs are shared among family members. In one study, 20 percent of Mexican farmworkers surveyed reported using injections, and 3.5 percent of them said they shared needles with their family.

Sharing syringes is a dangerous practice that puts many migrant families at risk of spreading disease.

thought of as an educational program, Migrant Head Start will be discussed in chapter 4, but it also offers numerous health benefits. Infants and young children are provided with standard health services such as immunizations. One study showed children of migrant farmworkers routinely received their immunizations "significantly later than the recommended schedule." Migrant Head Start also provides lead screenings. Health-care professionals who work with Head Start programs provide assessments of children's growth and development. This allows them to spot children suffering from malnutrition or with developmental delays. Other medical conditions can also be diagnosed and treated, or referrals for treatment can be made.

Some migrant families are eligible for Medicaid and other health insurance and service programs provided by the states where they temporarily live. However, many families are unaware of these programs or don't realize they could qualify for them. They may not know where to go to apply for services. When parents do not speak English or are not literate, they may not be capable of completing necessary forms. Other families cannot supply needed documentation. Even when families do apply, they sometimes move to other states before coverage takes effect. Or they may manage to enroll in state-funded health programs, but then find it difficult to find doctors who are taking new patients or to locate medical offices that operate during hours when workers can be away from their jobs.

Model Programs

Some *exemplary* programs exist where migrant families are well served by community health departments or other agencies that offer free or reduced-cost medical services, family planning, dental care, or pharmaceuticals. The Clinica Rural in Michigan is an example. Here, medical personnel and a van stocked with needed equip-

Picking fruit is backbreaking labor, but most migrant worker receive little if any medical care.

ment and supplies travel to migrant workers and their children rather than the other way around.

Rarely do health-care workers travel along the migrant stream to facilitate services to farmworker families. The Traveling Lay Health Advisor Project is one of the few projects that has operated in this manner. Conducted through the National Center for Farmworker Health, Inc., this program has allowed trained health advisers from Texas to travel the migrant stream, providing cancer education and health-care referrals to migrant women in fourteen other states. The Migrant Clinicians Network conducts health-related research and

Canadian Health Insurance

In Canada, each jurisdiction maintains its own comprehensive health insurance plan and may handle coverage of migrant workers in its own way. For example, migrant farmworkers in Ontario do not have to present residency documents to prove their eligibility for coverage. They also do not have to comply with the usual three-month waiting period for coverage to take effect. In Manitoba, however, nonresidents with work authorizations for less than one year are usually not eligible for insurance coverage.

acts as an advocate regarding health issues for migrant farmworkers and their families in the United States and Puerto Rico.

Wisconsin has developed a *reciprocity* agreement regarding Medicaid coverage for migrant farmworkers. If a worker qualifies for Medicaid in any state, he is accepted for coverage in Wisconsin. Wisconsin also bases eligibility on annual income. This is ideal, because sometimes the monthly income of a migrant farmworker can be high enough to disqualify him from Medicaid coverage.

:~~~:

The pesticides used on farm products can be dangerous to the workers who touch the plants over and over.

The nomadic lifestyle necessary for migrant farmworkers to obtain employment can be very hard on families. Children often do not receive the standard immunizations, making them vulnerable to childhood diseases such as measles and mumps. Nutritional deficiencies, common in migrant children, can cause complications in these and other conditions, as well as leave the youth susceptible to illness. Continuous *displacement* as children are moved from one school district to another complicates both health-care and the educational process.

CHAPTER 4
Education

Amalia's feet felt too heavy to lift as she climbed the wooden stairs of the trailer. Exhaustion seeped through every pore as she picked up her laptop and went online. She had been up since 4:00 A.M. when she helped her mother make lunches for the family. Now it was 6:30 P.M., and the family's lunch break was the only real free time she'd had. She was grateful when her mother said she didn't have to help make dinner. That would give her an extra hour to study before taking her math test. By working on schoolwork while in Illinois, Amalia would be on track to graduate with her class when she returned to Texas.

The Friends
We Don't Know

Imagine walking into a new school and discovering that, for every subject, students in your new classes use different books from what you used at your old school. Or if some of the same textbooks are used, your new classmates are at a different point in the curriculum. Maybe they've mastered math concepts that aren't familiar to you. You spend the next weeks trying to catch up, but it's not easy, especially since you work in the fields with your parents after school every weeknight and again on Saturday morning. Your parents don't speak English, so they can't help you. Even so, you do your best, and just when you're starting to feel like there may be hope, you find out your family is moving to a new state in two days.

It's easy to understand how struggles and disappointments like this can lead to dissatisfaction with school in general. No wonder the dropout rate for children of migrant farmworkers has reached twice that of others nationally.

Dislocation

Imagine playing a recurring role as the new kid in school, constantly being among the unfamiliar, never having time to bond with classmates or make close friends, always having to say good-bye. This is the life of some migrant kids who must change schools during the year. Even summer school programs may be disrupted as families move to seek continuing employment.

Language Issues

The enrollment of students with limited English *proficiency* rose to over 3.7 million in the 1999–2000 school year. Schools in many areas of the country may have difficulties offering bilingual or ESL (English as a Second Language) instruction. Without this, some migrant students may not be able to understand a teacher's instructions, read lessons, complete paperwork, or participate in classes.

A congressional study determined teachers often incorrectly perceive students with limited English proficiency to have lower academic abilities. Traditionally, migrant students have not been assigned to college-preparatory math and English classes.

Transferring Credits

Children who change schools frequently can suffer if their school records are not readily available to the new school. When prior work cannot be accessed, students may find themselves placed in inappropriate classes. Traditionally, migrant youths have had problems receiving credit for work accomplished in previous schools. When credits are not received, students can be held back and forced to repeat classes, even entire grades. This results in the child being older than others in the class. Such a child often ends up feeling uncomfortable and out of place.

Time Limitations

Migrant students often spend time after school and on weekends working in the fields. Their time for after-school activities, such as sports, is severely limited. This curtails their ability to bond with other students, to make lasting friendships, and to enjoy their school

The Migrant Education Program helps eligible children receive the educational services they need to learn.

experience. It also severely limits opportunities to develop a sense of community outside the family.

No Child Left Behind Act

Basically, the goal of the No Child Left Behind Act (NCLB) is to be certain all children in the United States are educated to their full potential, but some of its provisions are specific to migrant students. Through NCLB, the Department of Education is developing a national information system to facilitate electronic transfer of educational and health records for all children in the Migrant Education Program (MEP). NCLB also requires schools to provide migrant parents with student report cards "in a format and, to the extent practicable, in a language that they can understand."

If a child qualifies for specialized language instruction, his parents must be told why he qualifies, and they have the right to remove the child from such a program. Under NCLB, all teachers engaged in English instruction for students with limited English proficiency must be fluent in both English and any other language used in the program. States must establish standards, and schools must demonstrate that their curriculums effectively meet those standards.

The Migrant Education Program

First developed in 1966, this federal grant program helps qualifying migrant students between the ages of three and twenty-one succeed in school despite interruptions in school attendance. To qualify, children must have moved across school district boundaries to secure seasonal or temporary employment in an agricultural or fishing activity within the past thirty-six months. Or they have to have moved

Migrant Students Build Their Own School

The Great Depression of the 1930s brought an influx of more than 3 million people into the migrant stream, as farm families from dust-bowl areas were forced to leave their barren land and seek livelihoods elsewhere. Many sought agricultural work in California.

There, Leo Hart was superintendent of the Kern County School District. He lived next to one of the many camps set up as temporary housing for migrant families. Children living there told him of prejudices they faced in local schools. Adults in the district were trying to bar migrant children from school attendance altogether.

In response, Hart asked local businesses for donations of supplies, then organized some local teachers and fifty migrant students to build their own school at Weedpatch Camp. Though damaged in an earthquake in 1952, the school was rebuilt and still operates today as a public middle school, renamed Sunset School.

with a parent, guardian, or spouse during this time period and for this purpose. After their eligibility has been verified, migrant students qualify for MEP services for three years. MEPs operating in individual schools are required to:

- ensure special educational needs of migrant children are identified and addressed.

- provide migrant students with the opportunity to meet the same challenging state academic content standards that other children are expected to meet.

- promote interstate and intrastate coordination of services for migrant children, including educational continuity through the timely transfer of school records.

- encourage family literacy services for migrant students and their families.

- develop a written parent-involvement policy, stating the school's expectations for parental involvement, and distribute it to parents.

- invite and encourage parents to attend annual meetings held at convenient times for them.

- provide parents with a description of the school curriculum, information on academic assessment, and performance expectations for students.

- develop a school/parent compact that outlines how staff, students, and parents will share responsibility for improved student academic achievement (to the extent practicable, these materials must be in a format and language understandable to the parents).

- provide for outreach and *advocacy* for participating children and families regarding health, nutrition, education, and social services.

New Languages in North America

According to the Department of Health and Human Services, migrant health clinics in "many communities have begun to see greater numbers of families from rural Mexico and Central America who speak dialects unknown even by bilingual (Spanish/English) staff.

- provide family literacy programs.

- provide professional development programs for teachers and other program personnel.

- provide integration of information technology into program activities.

- provide programs to facilitate the transition of high school students to postsecondary education programs or employment.

Extended Day and Summer Programs

Don't you just love the idea of going to summer school? How about also working every day and then sandwiching classes into your only free time? That's what many migrant teens must do to graduate from high school. Yet many of these programs are innovative and provide unique opportunities.

A Sampling of Educational Opportunities for Migrant Youth

PORTABLE ASSISTANCE STUDY SEQUENCE (PASS)

In 1978, California became the first state to allow high school students to gain credits toward graduation through PASS. At least thirty states now offer migrant youth this alternative way of earning transferable high school credits. For each course, students engage in supervised self-directed study of various subjects, by completing a set of study units independently but under the direction of a teacher. Mini-PASS was developed in Wisconsin in 1985 to offer courses to students in grades six through eight.

COLLEGE ASSISTANCE MIGRANT PROGRAM (CAMP)

CAMP operates in six states and Puerto Rico. Through CAMP, migrant students who hope to pursue their education beyond high school can get an idea of what college life is like by attending summer programs on college campuses. CAMP helps migrant youth complete high school and prepare for college. It provides financial aid for the freshman year and helps students locate financial support for the remaining college years. A social network and academic support necessary for success are also provided through CAMP.

What's a GED?

Students who do not complete high school can earn their GED, which is the equivalent of a high school diploma. This certification allows them to apply to colleges and universities. It also makes them more prepared to enter the workforce if they do not choose to further their education.

ESTRELLA

This distance-learning program helped migrant students from six schools in Texas go from a 51 percent to a 92 percent graduation rate. Students in the program migrated to Illinois, Minnesota, Montana, and New York. The program supplied laptop computers and Internet service. Participants had access to local tutors, while college students served as "cyber-mentors."

MIGRANTS ACHIEVING SUCCESS (MAS+)

This is another example of a distance-learning program. It also supplies instructional support to migrant students through use of laptop computers and Internet access, thus allowing them to complete coursework and receive credits as they travel from their Texas-based schools. ESL classes are also offered.

HIGH SCHOOL EQUIVALENCY PROGRAM (HEP)

HEPs operate in twelve states and Puerto Rico. The goal of these programs is to help students earn their general equivalency diploma (GED) or a high school diploma.

A Model High School Program

A model program begun at one high school in 1998 ended with 77 percent of the 106 migrant seniors graduating in 2002. Of the remaining migrant students, 8 percent pursued their GED. Why did these students succeed? Staff was aggressive in meeting the students' needs:

- They created a culturally sensitive and welcoming environment in their office.

- They made students aware of the achievements of former migrant students who had graduated and gone on to college.

- They worked to develop home/school/community ties.

- They acted as mentors to students.

- They provided academic guidance so all necessary courses for graduation were completed.

- They provided tutors when necessary.

- They made sure students who lacked credits or needed to complete extra course work had access to summer programs.

Compulsory Schooling Laws in Canada

- New Brunswick: Children must attend school until they graduate from high school or reach age eighteen.

- Quebec: Children must attend school until the end of the school year for which they obtain a diploma issued by the Minister of Education, or until the end of the school year during which they turn sixteen.

- Other provinces: Students must attend until they turn sixteen.

- They helped students secure necessary resources, including computer equipment and Internet access so academic programs could be completed.

- They assisted students in finding appropriate after-school employment.

- They encouraged student participation in extracurricular and community activities.

- They provided college counseling.

Educational programs for migrant teens help them achieve both in school and out of it.

Mexican Students in the United States

The educational rights of Mexican children living in the United States were bolstered by a U.S. Supreme Court decision in 1982. In Plyer v. Doe, the Court ruled that undocumented children are entitled to both a public and a bilingual education as well as free and reduced-price lunches and other programs that promote success in school.

A Model Preschool Program

As the name implies, the goal of Migrant Head Start is to provide services to preschool-aged children and their parents so the children will be well prepared for success when they enter school. Migrant parents who have access to Head Start have a safe place for their infants, toddlers, and young children through the age of five during working hours. They no longer have to leave them in the care of older children or bring them to the field.

Transportation can be a difficult barrier for migrant families. Migrant Head Start programs often operate vans or buses that travel miles of rural roads to pick up and return young clients. Personnel are often bilingual. Structured play that promotes creativity and literacy can be designed to reflect children's cultural backgrounds. Young children can go on field trips, thereby experiencing local sites their parents don't have time to visit. Meals and snacks are provided. Parents are consulted and apprised of their children's needs and progress, thus setting the tone for parental involvement in their child's educational future.

Despite the many health and education programs designed for their benefit, migrant children and youth are still considered by many to be among the most disadvantaged young people in the United States. Some of the reasons for this can be found in housing and mental health issues.

CHAPTER 5
Housing, Mental Health, & Other Issues

In her book *Barefoot Heart: Stories of a Migrant Child*, author Elva Treviño Hart explains she only felt shame once regarding the life she and her family led as migrant workers. That was when, as an adult, she discovered that the stop-sign-shaped home provided to her family during the summers they worked in Minnesota had previously been used as a sow *farrowing* shed.

Housing

According to the NAWS, 21 percent of migrant farmworkers live in free housing that is provided by their employer. Another 7 percent rent housing from their employer, while the rest find housing elsewhere.

1983 Migrant and Seasonal Agricultural Workers Protection Act

This law established standards the Occupational Safety and Health Administration (OSHA) must follow as it regulates farm-worker housing.

Sometimes housing is provided in the form of "labor camps." This type of housing often consists of one- and two-bedroom units. Floors may be cement. A one-bedroom unit might house four people, and a two-bedroom unit might be home for as many as ten. Most standard units have kitchen facilities. Basic major appliances such as refrigerators and ranges are furnished, along with a dining table, chairs, and beds or mattresses. Each housing unit may have a bathroom, but often showers and bathroom facilities will be located elsewhere and shared with other workers. When *communal* showers are provided, there might not be enough hot water for everyone. Air conditioning is a luxury most migrant families do without, but fans are sometimes provided.

When growers provide housing, it is supposed to be inspected and meet federal standards. Sometimes it is not inspected on schedule, leading to abuses of the law. When growers are unable or unwilling to bring substandard housing up to regulations, it may be closed down. Ironically, one of the results of this attempt to improve living conditions for farmworkers is that many growers have ceased providing housing, creating a housing shortage. This has forced many to seek housing in low-income areas, to pay high rents for limited housing, or to move in with others to save money. Many families find temporary housing in trailer parks. Unfortunately, some housing is unsanitary, unsafe, does not have appliances that work, does not have functioning plumbing, does not protect inhabitants from inclement weather, is infested with vermin such as cockroaches and mice, or is located in the most polluted parts of towns.

According to the Housing Assistance Council (HAC), over 26 percent of migrant housing units in one survey were located adjacent to fields that had been sprayed with pesticides, yet more than half of these units were without a washing machine or a functioning bathtub or shower. When plumbing does not work properly, people may not be able to shower after work. When a washing machine is not available, they might have to resort to wearing clothing already contaminated with agricultural residue. When housing is not structurally sound or has exposed electrical wiring, inhabitants can be injured or fires can occur. When old paint is peeling off walls, children may be exposed to lead. High levels of lead can cause severe damage, but even low levels can decrease a child's IQ and the development of his motor functions. When appliances don't work, food can spoil or families can be deprived of warm meals. When rodents or insects get into a house, they contaminate food and might bite residents. Conditions like this can lead to the spread of infectious disease. Fifty-seven percent of the migrant housing units the HAC surveyed in Florida were found to be substandard, with 31 percent of those labeled "severely" substandard.

The HAC found 52 percent of migrant housing units were crowded. Of the crowded units, 74 percent housed children along with adult residents. In some areas, one-bedroom trailers housed up to a dozen people. Overcrowding means occupants may have to sleep on mattresses placed on the floor. Sometimes mattresses must be shared. Other times even mattresses are unavailable. Not having a decent bed can add to the suffering of those who strain their

Housing Regulations in Canada

Free housing for migrant farmworkers in Canada must be provided, and it has to include: either a kitchen with cooking facilities or meals, two bedrooms or a bedroom and a living room, and a private toilet and washing facilities. Additionally, the employer must furnish heat, electricity, and water.

muscles every day in the field. Children need their sleep to develop properly.

Sometimes migrant workers are unable to locate or afford any housing. Steven Greenhouse reported on conditions like this in a 1998 article published in the *New York Times*. In "As U.S. Economy Booms, Migrant Workers Housing Worsens," he called attention to migrant workers inhabiting garages and toolsheds; some even resorted to living in caves. According to Greenhouse, **squatter** camps had arisen in some areas, consisting of makeshift housing composed of scraps of wood, plastic, and cardboard. In describing conditions in Immokalee, Florida, Greenhouse noted migrant youth and their families living in trailers that had their exteriors painted to give the impression of upkeep but that lacked work on the inside. According to the article, ceilings were crisscrossed with electrical wires. Vermin were also a problem: "To protect their food supplies from rats, migrants hang bags of flour and cornmeal, piñata-like, from strings nailed to the ceiling."

When migrant farmworkers depart for new areas of the country, they are often unsure of where their next temporary home will be. Migrant families unable to locate housing but lucky enough to own their own vehicle may sometimes sleep in it, or they may rent a hotel room.

Mental Health Issues

The instability of not knowing where your next home or job will be combined with economic hardship and isolation posed by a transient lifestyle can cause stress. Being far from the emotional support of friends and extended family can add to that stress. Issues of discrimination or feeling powerless can *exacerbate* the situation. Isolation caused by a language barrier and a host of other negatives, such as having to do hard physical labor without enough time off, can compound these difficulties. For some individuals, all these stresses may contribute to mental health problems.

Occasional anxiety and depression are normal parts of life, but when these conditions grow in severity or become chronic, they can be very serious. One study that measured the risk of developing depression among migrant farmworkers who were also mothers found 41 percent of them were at significant risk. When mothers are depressed, their condition naturally impacts their children.

Another study determined that migrant farmworkers were at a 10 percent greater risk of developing anxiety-related illnesses than the general population. People with anxiety disorders might not be able to concentrate well or may worry constantly. Children and youth who are so burdened might feel tense and panicky. They may find it increasingly difficult to sleep, become prone to bursts of anger, have eating disorders, or develop other serious health problems such as heart disease. If their parents have anxiety disorders, migrant youth may not feel the security necessary for the development of high self-esteem.

Substance Abuse/Child Abuse

Several studies have found substance abuse among male migrant farmworkers to be above the national average. Substance abuse can lead to domestic violence.

A study conducted in five states in 1990 determined children of migrant workers were three times more likely than other children residing in those states to become victims of neglect or other forms of child abuse. A study conducted in New York found incidents of migrant child maltreatment were six times higher than the state average.

One study involving eight- through eleven-year-old children of African American and Mexican migrant farmworkers showed 8 percent of the kids were depressed. Over 50 percent of the children exhibited some form of anxiety, and 17 percent of them engaged in disruptive behaviors. People, including children and youth, with severe anxiety or depression may have thoughts of suicide.

To alleviate stress, anxiety, and depression, some people resort to using alcohol or other drugs. This can result in addiction—and people with addictions may engage in dangerous behaviors. Substance abuse can also cause serious physical health problems.

Many farmworkers face prejudice based on the color of their skin.

A History of Racism and Segregation

Prior to the civil rights movement, many people of Mexican or African descent, including migrant workers, were victimized by segregationist policies. They were forced to ride at the back of buses, to use special entrances and to sit in designated areas of restaurants, refused access to parks and swimming areas, relegated to specified seating in theaters, and otherwise restricted in public places. These children and youths often had to attend segregated schools or, at least, segregated classrooms.

Bridging the Cultural Divide in Leamington, Ontario

This city, located near Detroit, Michigan, is considered by many to be the center of Canada's hothouse tomato industry. Each year, approximately 2,500 Mexican migrant guest workers call Leamington home. Canadian residents of Leamington donate used bicycles to these workers so they have independent transportation, and St. Michael's Catholic Church has instituted a Spanish-language mass to serve their religious needs.

In the 1930s, migrants from Oklahoma were sometimes called "maggots." Children who were better off financially laughed at these students because of their tattered appearance. Since the 1960s, the United States has made tremendous strides in combating segregation and inequality, yet even today an undercurrent of racism sometimes reveals itself.

In 1999, workers at a Migrant and Seasonal Head Start program in Tennessee wanted to open another center in a neighboring county. Approximately 400 of the 600 community residents opposed the new center and signed a petition against it. More than 100 people participated in a protest march. Protesters referred to the migrant workers whose children would benefit from the center as "illegal aliens."

Signs such as "No way, José" appeared on town buildings. Someone ran two Head Start buses off the road. A barn located on land that was to be used for the facility was set on fire. A stuffed dummy smeared with ketchup was discovered on the landlord's property. These violent and threatening acts were considered hate crimes and led to an FBI investigation. Some community members supported the planned facility and spoke in its favor at a public meeting. The Migrant Head Start project went forward and has operated in the community without incident. Unfortunately, people are often opposed to construction of housing or location of services for migrant workers in their neighborhoods.

The Neighbors We Haven't Met

Most local community residents and migrant families do not interact. Migrant workers often are not noticed. Even those who return to the same farms year after year usually have little interaction with area residents. Few residents realize migrant families bring a boost to local economies.

Caught in a Cycle of Poverty

Wages paid to farm laborers are low. The larger the family is, the more hands available for picking so the larger the combined family income. This is why many parents depend on their children to assist in earning this seasonal money. Even so, approximately 70 percent of migrant farmworker children live below the poverty level. Another cause of poverty is that many migrant farmworkers are

César Chávez—From Migrant Child to Internationally Known Leader

Beginning in the 1960s, under the courageous and creative leadership of César Chávez, the United Farmworkers organized strikes and boycotts leading to improved wages and working conditions for many agricultural laborers. His wife, Helen, and their friend, Dolores Huerta, were other leaders in the movement.

Though César Chávez lived the typical transient life of migrant children of his time, attending thirty-seven schools before dropping out after the eighth grade, he went on to earn the admiration and respect of millions. He was presented with the Martin Luther King Nonviolent Peace Award in 1974.

César Chávez died in 1993. Befitting the humility he modeled to others in life, he was buried in a plain pine casket. Approximately forty thousand mourners participated in the funeral procession. Honoring the leader, California has adopted the first paid state holiday in his name and developed a model school curriculum on his life and work.

unable to locate consistent employment. According to the NAWS, many migrant farmworkers find employment for only seventeen weeks out of the year.

Although many migrant families feel forced to ask their children to participate in farm labor, most of these parents do not want their children to follow in their footsteps. They realize education can mean new opportunities and see it as the key to finding employment that will allow their children to break out of a cycle of poverty.

Over the years, many educational, health, housing, and other programs have been developed to assist migrant families, yet thousands remain underserved. One problem concerns funding. Programs have been plagued with a consistent lack of funds needed to operate at full potential.

CHAPTER 6
Recapping Major Hurdles Faced by Migrant Youth

On seeing the television documentary *Harvest of Shame*, which aired on Thanksgiving Day in 1960, the American public was shocked to learn of the living and working conditions of migrant farmworkers. Despite the commitment demonstrated during the ensuing forty-plus years by advocates, educators, and health and social service providers, gaps in services delivered to migrant farmworker families still exist. According to the NAWS, only 17 percent of migrant families take advantage of social services such as food stamps, Medicaid, welfare, or Temporary Assistance to Needy Families.

Health Barriers

Despite efforts to provide migrant families with necessary health care, the need for primary and preventative health care continues. An article titled "Access to Care for Children of Migratory Agricultural Workers: Factors Associated with Unmet Need for Medical Care" appeared in the April 2004 issue of *PEDIATRICS*. According to the article, in a 1999 survey, 300 migrant adult caretakers indicated 53 percent of their children under age thirteen had an unmet medical need during the past year. That is twenty-four times greater than the unmet medical needs of children in the general population.

Much of this need was attributable to a lack of transportation or to not knowing where to seek medical care. Many families did not own a vehicle and were dependent on others for transportation. Lack of public transportation in rural areas contributes to the problem. According to the article, "Female gender, preschool age, and high caretaker work pressure were directly associated with unmet medical need." More than half of the caretakers said they feared job loss if they took time off to take their child to the doctor.

More than a third of the children had never had a routine physical, and for just over half of the children, more than three years had gone by since their last well-child examination. Almost 80 percent of these children had never had a dental exam. Yet each of the four counties involved in the survey had a health facility and a county health department. Only one lacked a hospital with an emergency room. Two had migrant health centers. In other words, though medical care was available, many migrant families were not aware it was there, or they were not able to travel to the facilities.

Other organizations point out the need for a reliable national database to store and transfer medical records of migrant workers and their family members. According to the Migrant Clinicians Network, "There is probably no other population in the United

States that has had simultaneously high incidences of both over immunization and under immunization in children." This is due to poor record keeping. The NCFH says, "The migratory lifestyle, language barriers, poor living conditions, and a lack of sufficient financial resources or health insurance make access to health care and the continuity of care incredibly difficult" for migrant farmworkers and their children.

Education Barriers

The children of settled migrants and shuttle migrants are ineligible for MEPs unless they have moved to a new school district because of agricultural employment within the past three years. In 1994, Congress passed the Improving America's Schools Act, which changed eligibility requirements for MEPs. Prior to this change, students could participate within six years of having migrated. Changing the requirements disqualified approximately 200,000 children.

Locating children and youth who could qualify for programs can be difficult. School recruiters, for example, might only find children who are already enrolled in such programs. Children of undocumented workers may be avoiding detection. Other times, programs like Migrant Head Start are overbooked, and children on waiting lists are unable to receive needed services.

The mobile lifestyle of migrant children and youth has always led to confusion regarding accurate and up-to-date health and education records. Over the years, many students did not receive course credit because of recording problems. This sometimes kept them from graduating on time or caused them to be unable to keep up with the advancement of their classmates to new grades.

Distance-learning programs are now helping many migrant students complete their high school education. Some programs supply

Ask Yourself

- Is leaving farm employment the only way for migrant families to break out of the poverty cycle? If they do that, who will grow and harvest North America's food?

- How would you encourage children and teens to seek the friendship of migrant students who become the "new kids" in their schools?

- Does being patriotic mean we should look down on illegal immigrants?

CD-ROMs with bilingual curriculums that can be completed in school. Other programs provide lessons through special televisions or by way of laptop computers provided to students. Donations of equipment and services can help alleviate costs; still, the money needed for some hi-tech programs can be *prohibitive*. In "For Migrant Kids, Laptop Is Lifeline," *Chicago Tribune* reporter Oscar Avila put the cost of the ESTRELLA program at "about $8,000 per participant."

According to John Bailey, the director of educational technology for the U.S. Department of Education's Enhancing Education Through Technology program, part of the nation's No Child Left Behind agenda, $700 million is available for qualifying school programs, and some of these funds could be used for migrant education. Some surveys, however, report as many as two-thirds of America's teachers do not feel prepared to use computers for instruction.

In 2004, the federal government cut funding for the Migrant and Seasonal Farmworker Youth Program in thirty-one states and Puerto Rico. This program, aimed at reversing the dropout rate among migrant students, had funded more than 2,500 youths between the ages of fourteen and twenty-one the previous year. It had supplied tutors and other resources and also replaced income lost to parents when children remained in school rather than worked in agriculture.

Inadequate Housing

Problems associated with providing affordable housing to migrant families continue to grow as land prices and construction costs escalate. When farmers or other landlords receive rent money only for part of the year, how can they build properties that demand mortgage payments throughout the year, and how can they keep monthly rents low enough for migrant families to afford them?

A 2004 Associated Press article documents the continuing scarcity of housing for Oregon's migrant laborers. According to the article, some migrant farmworkers "sleep in cars, barns or under bridges. Others inhabit rustic farm labor camps. And some take up in homeless shelters." Yet despite the housing shortage migrant farmworkers face across the nation, funds that could support the construction of migrant housing are being cut. A 2005 Associated Press article laments the plan of Michigan governor Jennifer Grantholm to cut $255,000 from that state's Migrant Housing Labor Grant program. According to a spokesperson for Michigan's Department of Management and Budget, the cut was necessary due to a $773 million shortfall in the state budget.

Mental Health

Poor wages, substandard housing, difficult working conditions, and an inability to obtain necessary medical services combine to place migrant families among those with the lowest standard of living in the United States and place them in danger of developing depression or an anxiety disorder. Studies indicate children of first-generation migrant workers are at greater risk for developing these conditions than are their immigrant parents. In "Mental Health and Substance Abuse," Joseph D. Hovey discusses possible reasons for this. According to Dr. Hovey:

> Immigrant workers may compare their current life situations to a lower socioeconomic experience in Mexico, whereas second and greater generation workers—who tend to be more educated—may be more sensitive to the discrepancy between their current life conditions and those of others in the U.S.

It may be *imperative* for second-generation migrant farmworkers to move beyond this type of employment. According to an Associated Press article published in 2005, however, President Bush "wants to eliminate the National Farmworker Jobs Program, which gives migrant workers the training and support they need to get jobs as nurses assistants, dental technicians and in other professions." In the past, when President Bush has wanted the program eliminated, Congress has acted to restore funding.

Illegal Immigrants

Fear of deportation can prevent parents without proper documentation from enrolling their children in schools or health-care programs. *Disdain* for illegal immigrants (and possibly other immigrants) seems to be rising.

In 1994, California voters passed Proposition 187. Under this law, rights to health care and education were to be denied to people without documents to prove they were in the country legally. Educators and other school personnel were to report undocumented youth to the U.S. Citizenship and Naturalization Services. The Immigration Act of 1996 prohibited states from passing their own immigration laws, thus opening the way for the federal district court in Los Angeles to rule Proposition 187 unconstitutional.

In 2004, Arizona voters passed Proposition 200, also known as the Taxpayer and Citizen Protection Act. Under this law, state workers can request proof of legal status when people apply for state services and are to report illegal residents to immigration officials. If the state workers do not, they can face a fine or up to four months in jail. Some migrant workers without documentation have children who were born in the United States. In fact, 73 percent of the children of foreign-born migrant workers were born in the United States, making these children citizens. But undocumented workers fear their children could lose their benefits because of this law.

Child Labor

Although child labor laws exist, they are not always enforced. The large number of farms hiring seasonal workers makes policing difficult, and many farmers do not take the time to check documents proving the ages of youths who wish to work.

A complicated set of issues surrounds migrant children and youth. In order to prevent this important segment of society from "falling between the cracks," we must ask ourselves some tough questions.

CHAPTER 7
Food for Thought:
Issues for Class Discussion

Farmworkers have played a critical role in North America for more than a century. The desperation of small farmers during the Great Depression forced them to sell their land and presented an opportunity for wealthy landowners to acquire vast amounts of it. Instead of one small farmer growing a variety of crops, agriculture has steadily evolved to fewer landowners with each farm growing fewer types of crops. Changing agricultural methods also played a role in the evolution of migrant labor. As the development of farm machinery progressed, the need for laborers at various points in the planting cycle changed. For many crops, fewer workers are now necessary. Sometimes farmers hire only a few migrant workers to operate machinery necessary to plant, tend, or harvest crops. Farmworkers are hired just for the amount of time needed to perform a specified job—the summer, only a month or a week, even just a day. This has led to the nomadic nature of farmwork today.

Every U.S. state and many provinces in Canada have seasonal migrant workers. Yet many of us have not thought much about our dependence on this group of dedicated workers. Here are some questions to consider:

- Is it okay for a fourteen-year-old to perform farm labor?

- Is it okay for a fourteen-year-old to work on the migrant trail?

- No matter how hard he tries, a father of four is unable to find consistent employment in their Texas town. Because of their financial situation, the family lives in the home of relatives. That family also has children, so it is very crowded. If the father, his wife, and all four of their children spend a few years working together as migrant farmworkers and pool the money earned, they will be able to afford to purchase building materials for a house. The father sometimes does construction work, so he plans to build the house himself during the months the family is in Texas. Should they embark on the migrant labor circuit?

- Would your family be willing to pay five cents more for a head of lettuce so farmworkers who harvested the lettuce would have a higher income?

- Would you be willing to pay five cents more for each item purchased at the grocery store?

- Do you think some families in North America would suffer if the cost of food were raised five cents per item?

When we buy our fruit and vegetables, how many of us remember the many human hands that picked that fruit?

- Are you familiar with the Migrant Education Program in your school or state? How many students does it serve and what types of support and services does it offer?

- Have you ever worked in an agricultural field?

- If wages paid to harvesters increased, do you think more local residents in your area would like to do this work?

- If wages for farmworkers increased, might enough local workers be available so that migrant workers would be unnecessary?

Beyond NAFTA

Although Canada, the United States, and Mexico have a free-trade agreement (NAFTA), all three countries restrict the flow of laborers across borders. Former Mexican president Vincente Fox wanted to see the United States institute a broad temporary-worker program so more agricultural laborers and some others would be able to cross the U.S. border legally for employment purposes.

- Remembering that the majority of these workers have a sixth-grade education, how might those working within the migrant streams make a living if migrant labor were to disappear?

- Do you believe it is right to provide an education for children who are not citizens while their parents are working as migrant farmworkers in the United States?

- How might the United States benefit if citizens of Mexico receive part of their education in the United States?

- How close is the nearest agricultural area to your home or school? Are you aware of the types of pesticides, herbicides, or fungicides used there? Do you think you have a right to know when chemicals are being used on local fields?

Glossary

advocacy: Active support for a cause or position.

chronic: Long term or recurring frequently.

cilantro: The leaves of the coriander plant, used especially in Latin and Southwest U.S. cooking.

communal: Used or owned by all members of a group or community.

communicable: Capable of passing between persons.

deportation: The forcible expulsion of a foreign national from a country.

disdain: Extreme contempt or disgust for something or someone.

displacement: The act of moving a person away from his or her normal home.

emancipated minors: Children under the age of legal adulthood who the court has made independent.

exacerbate: Make worse.

exemplary: Deserving imitation because of excellence.

farrowing: Giving birth to piglets.

fungicides: Chemicals used to stop plant diseases caused by fungi.

herbicides: Chemicals used to kill weeds.

imperative: Absolutely necessary.

infant mortality rate: The number of deaths during the first year of life per thousand live births.

Mennonites: Members of a Protestant group emphasizing adult baptism and pacifism and rejecting church organizations and, sometimes, the holding of public office and the swearing of oaths.

otitis media: Inflammation of the middle ear, marked by pain, fever, dizziness, and hearing abnormalities.

proficiency: Skill.

prohibitive: Preventing something from happening.

reciprocity: A relationship involving mutual exchange.

squatter: An illegal occupant of land or property.

stereotypes: Generalizations based on incomplete and often erroneous information.

transient: Moving from place to place.

trauma: Injury.

Further Reading

Altman, Linda Jacobs. *Migrant Farm Workers: The Temporary People*. New York: Franklin Watts, 2004.

Atkin, S. Beth. *Voices From the Fields: Children of Migrant Farmworkers Tell Their Stories*. New York: Scholastic, 2003.

Buirski, Nancy. *Earth Angels: Migrant Children in America*. San Francisco, Calif.: Pomegranate Art Books, 2004.

Ferris, Susan, Ricardo Sandoval, Diana Hembree, and Michele McKenzie. *The Fight in the Fields: Cesar Chavez and the Farmworkers Movement*. New York: Harcourt Brace & Company, 1997.

Garza, Encarnacion, Pedro Reyes, and Enrique T. Trueba. *Resiliency and Success: Migrant Children in the U.S.* Boulder, Colo.: Paradigm Publishers, 2004.

Hart, Elva Traviño. *Barefoot Heart: Stories of a Migrant Child*. Tempe, Ariz.: Bilingual Press, 1999.

Hovius, Christopher. *Latino Migrant Workers: America's Harvesters*. Broomall, Pa.: Mason Crest Publishers, 2005.

Hoyt-Goldsmith, D. *Migrant Worker: A Boy from the Rio Grande Valley*. New York: Holiday House, 2000.

Jimenez, Francisco. *The Circuit: Stories from the Life of a Migrant Child*. Albuquerque: University of New Mexico Press, 1997.

Libal, Autumn. *Women in the Hispanic World*. Broomall, Pa.: Mason Crest Publishers Inc., 2005.

Martinez, Ruben. *Crossing Over: A Mexican Family on the Migrant Trail*. New York: Metropolitan Books, 2001.

Rothenberg, Daniel. *With These Hands: The Hidden World of Migrant Workers Today*. New York: Harcourt Brace & Company, 1998.

Valle, Isabel. *Fields of Toil: A Migrant Family's Journey*. Pullman: Washington State University Press. 2004.

Wiggins, Melinda, and Charles D. Thompson (editors). *The Human Cost of Food: Farmworkers' Lives, Labor, and Advocacy*. Austin: University of Texas Press, 2002.

For More Information

Canada's Migrant Workers
www.justicia4migrantworkers.org/resources.htm

César Chávez and the United Farm Workers
www.ufw.org/

Migrant Farmworker History, Statistics, and Lesson Plans
www.farmworkers.cornell.edu/curriculum.htm

Migrant Oral Histories
www.accd.edu/pac/history/hist1302/OralHistoryMigrants.htm
score.rims.k12.ca.us/score_lessons/chavez/pages/introduction.html

Migrant Scholarships
www.migrant.net/scholaship.htm

Migrant Student Success Stories
www.migrant.net.pass/success/success.htm

Office of Migrant Education
www.ed.gov/offices/OESE/MEP

Overview of Services offered at the Geneseo Migrant Center in New York State
www.migrant.net/services.htm

Picture History of Migrant Workers
www.picturehistory.com/search?word1=migrant+workers&submitx=
11&submit.y=7

Quality Education for Minorities Network
qemnetwork.qem.org

Scholarship Opportunities for Hispanic Students
www.HispanicScholarship.com

Student Eligibility Requirements for the Migrant Education Program
www.ice-com.com/sccoe/english/studenteligibility.html

Title/Author Booklist
www.migrantlibrary.org/list.asp?Type=Title

Publisher's note:
The Web sites listed on this page were active at the time of publication. The publisher is not responsible for Web sites that have changed their addresses or discontinued operation since the date of publication. The publisher will review and update the Web-site list upon each reprint.

Bibliography

Coles, Robert. *Uprooted Children: The Early Life of Migrant Farm Workers.* Pittsburgh, Pa.: University of Pittsburgh Press, 1970.

Employment Standards Fact Sheet—Agricultural Workers/Ontario Ministry of Labor. 2005. http://www.gov.on.ca/LAB/english/es/factsheets/fs_agri.html.

Gouwens, Judith A. *Migrant Education: A Reference Handbook.* Santa Barbara, Calif.: ABC-CLIO, Inc. 2001.

National Children's Center for Rural and Agricultural Health and Safety. 2005. http://research.marshfieldclinic.org/children/Resources/Agriculture/ FactSheet.htm

Index

Picture Credits

Craig, Heather/Fotolia: p. 45
iStockphoto: pp. 33, 41, 52, 71
    Barley, Sean: p. 64
    Clark, Anne: p. 18
    Frank, Glenn: pp. 14, 84
    Gearhart, Rosemarie: p. 76
    Hahn, Tom: p. 87
    Nehring, Nancy: p. 10
    Rinaldi, Giovanni: p. 30
    Seeden, Lynn: p. 61
    Stalb, Pattie: p. 8
    Steib, Patty: p. 27
    Stewart, Brian: p. 43
    Walker, Duncan: p. 48
    Wallis, Sally: p. 39
MOKreations: p. 47

To the best knowledge of the publisher, all other images are in the public domain. If any image has been inadvertently uncredited, please notify Harding House Publishing Service, Vestal, New York 13850, so that rectification can be made for future printings.

Biographies

Author

Joyce Libal is a graduate of the University of Wisconsin. In addition to having worked as a magazine editor, she has written several books for adolescents. Joyce and her family have enjoyed raising many pets including chickens, geese, rabbits, dogs, cats, horses, and a pony on their Pennsylvania farm.

Series Consultant

Celeste J. Carmichael is a 4-H Youth Development Program Specialist at the Cornell University Cooperative Extension Administrative Unit in Ithaca, New York. She provides leadership to statewide 4-H Youth Development efforts including communications, curriculum, and conferences. She communicates the needs and impacts of the 4-H program to staff and decision makers, distributing information about issues related to youth and development, such as trends for rural youth.